Published by Ladybird Books Ltd
A Penguin Company
Penguin Books Ltd, 80 Strand, London WC2R 0RL, UK
Penguin Books Australia Ltd, 707 Collins Street, Melbourne, Victoria 3008, Australia
Penguin Group (NZ) 67 Apollo Drive, Rosedale, North Shore 0632, New Zealand

001

© Ladybird Books Limited MMXIII

Text © Judith Nicholls MMIII

ISBN: 978-0-72327-152-9

Printed in China

Published by Ladybird Books Ltd
A Penguin Company
Penguin Books Ltd, 80 Strand, London WC2R 0RL, UK
Penguin Books Australia Ltd, 707 Collins Street, Melbourne, Victoria 3008, Australia
Penguin Group (NZ) 67 Apollo Drive, Rosedale, North Shore 0632, New Zealand

001

© Ladybird Books Limited MMXIII

Text © Judith Nicholls MMIII

ISBN: 978-0-72327-152-9

Printed in China

Ladybird
I'm Ready...to Read!

Trip-Trot Tippy Toes

written by Judith Nicholls ★ illustrated by Emilie Chollat

"I'm a trip-trot, leap-a-lot, skipping, hopping hare."

"Race me, Owl!
Chase me, Fox!
Catch me if
you dare!"

"Oh do be quiet, Hare!" said Owl.
"I'm trying to take a sleep."

8

"Just watch me trip and hop," yelled Hare,
"and prance and dance and leap!"

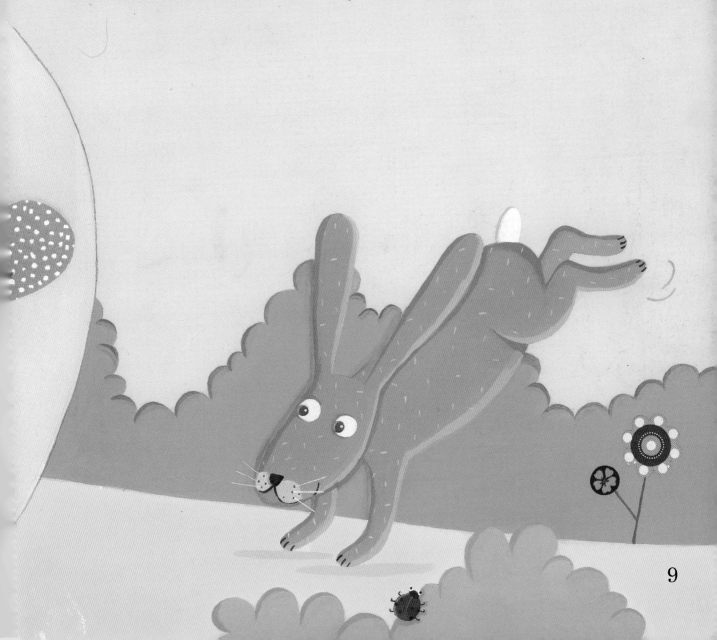

"Oh do be quiet!" Squirrel cried.
"You're such a show-off, Hare."

10

"I'm sure that Fox could beat you, or Tortoise over there!"

11

Tortoise woke up with a start.

"What, that old lazy-lump?
I'll trip-trot to the moon and back
the day I see him jump!"

13

"Race him, Tortoise!" Squirrel cried.
"We've heard all this before!"

"Race him, Tiptoe Tortoise, please! We know you're slow but sure!"

"I'm a dance-a-lot, prance-a-lot, skipping hopping hare!"

16

Hare bounded loudly from the start,
left Tortoise standing there.

Tortoise set off, slow but sure,
towards the shady wood.
He tramped along on tippy-toes;
he'd do the best he could!

18

19

Hare darted past the oak trees
and past the sycamore.
He darted through the ferns
that lined the forest floor.

The day was hot and very soon
he reached a mossy gap.
"That tortoise must be miles behind,
I'll take a little nap!"

The Tiptoe Tortoise toddled on.
He could not win this race.

"Come on, you're slow but sure," cried Owl.
"Just keep that steady pace."

Much later on he reached the gap where Hare slept in the sun.

A wide smile spread across his face.
"That hare has not yet won!"

The Trip-Trot Hare woke with a start;
he dreamt he'd won the race.

And then he saw the Tiptoe Tortoise...

...slow but sure,
sat at the winning place!

29

Look out for...

Ladybird I'm Ready...to Read!

Rhythm and Rhyme Stories

Snick-Snack Sniffle-Nose

Ladybird I'm Ready...to Read!

Rhythm and Rhyme Stories

Knock! Knock!

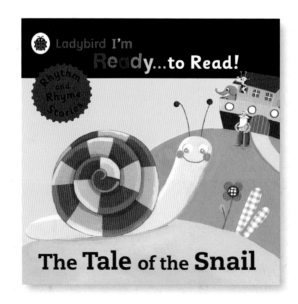

Ladybird I'm Ready...to Read!

Rhythm and Rhyme Stories

The Tale of the Snail